P9-ELX-581

ELLA, of course!

WRITTEN BY Sarah Weeks

ILLUSTRATED BY Doug Cushman

Harcourt, Inc.
Orlando   Austin   New York   San Diego   Toronto   London

Requests for permission to make copies of any part of the work should be submitted online
at www.harcourt.com/contact or mailed to the following address: Permissions Department,
Harcourt, Inc., 6277 Sea Harbor Drive, Orlando, Florida 32887-6777.

www.HarcourtBooks.com

Library of Congress Cataloging-in-Publication Data
Weeks, Sarah.
Ella, of course/Sarah Weeks; illustrated by Doug Cushman.
p. cm.
Summary: When Ella is banned from bringing her umbrella to the dance recital, she
comes up with an ingenious solution to the problem.
[1. Problem solving—Fiction. 2. Umbrellas—Fiction. 3. Dance recitals—Fiction.
4. Ballet dancing—Fiction.] I. Cushman, Doug, ill. II. Title.
PZ7.W42215Ell 2007
[E]—dc22   2005025910
ISBN 978-0-15-204943-0

First edition
A C E G H F D B

Printed in Singapore

The illustrations in this book were done in acrylic on
Arches watercolor paper prepared with gesso.
The display lettering was created by Kirsten Horel.
The text type was set in Mercurius medium.
Color separations by Bright Arts Ltd., Hong Kong
Printed and bound by Tien Wah Press, Singapore
This book was printed on totally chlorine-free Stora Enso Matte paper.
Production supervision by Jane Van Gelder
Designed by Lydia D'moch

À Florence, qui, comme Ella,
apprécie un parapluie fidèle
—S. W.

To Gerald McDermott,
colleague, mentor, and friend
—D. C.

Ella was a problem solver. When one of Aunt Mozelle's favorite earrings fell down the drain, who do you suppose got it out with a high-heeled shoe and a wad of bubblegum? Ella, of course.

When Ella's little brother's pet frog, Sylvio, escaped and interrupted the neighbor's Hawaiian pool party, who do you suppose got him back with the help of a spaghetti strainer and a curtain rod?

Ella, of course.

On Ella's fourth birthday, her grammy sent her a present. Inside the long skinny box was...

... AN UMBRELLA!

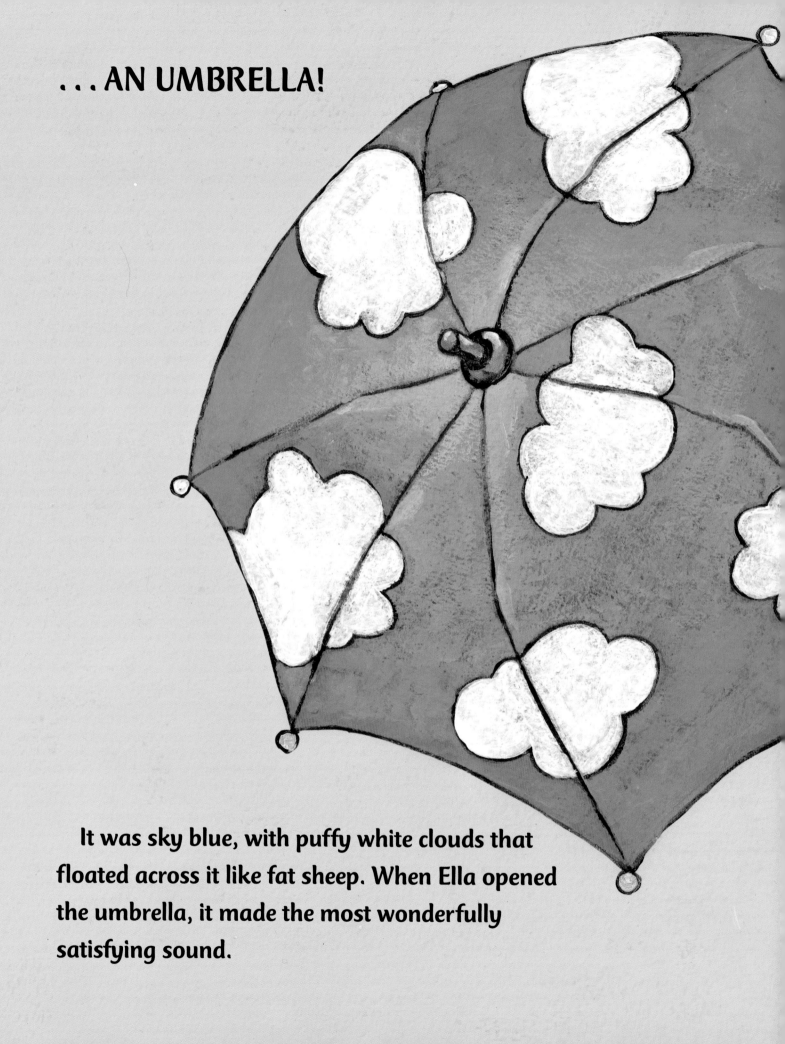

It was sky blue, with puffy white clouds that floated across it like fat sheep. When Ella opened the umbrella, it made the most wonderfully satisfying sound.

WHOOSH...click!

WHOOSH...click!

Ella love-love-*loved* her new umbrella. She loved it so much, she took it with her everywhere she went. But everywhere she went, now instead of solving problems she *caused* them.

Who do you suppose brought her umbrella to school—
and caused a soggy problem at show-and-tell?
Ella, of course.

And who do you suppose brought her umbrella to the grocery store—and caused a sticky problem in aisle three? Ella, of course.

Ella took her umbrella to ballet class, too, and caused such a BIG problem that Mrs. LaTouche made her put it in the corner until the class was over.

"Don't forget—the dance recital is this Friday!"
Mrs. LaTouche called after the little ballerinas
as they left. "Parents are welcome, but in case
anyone is wondering, umbrellas are *not*."

Who do you suppose had been
planning to bring her umbrella
to the recital?
Ella, of course.

Ella was nervous about dancing in front of a lot of people. She just knew that if she could have her umbrella with her, she wouldn't be afraid. What was she going to do now?

Toys

Lately, Ella had been very busy causing problems and having problems, but that didn't mean she had forgotten who she was, for heaven's sake: Ella was a problem solver. So she went to look for a good pair of scissors and a hunk of old garden hose.

At the recital on Friday, the audience sat politely and quietly. But the minute the curtains opened, everyone began to whisper and point.

"Who is leaping higher than all the rest?"

"Who doesn't look the least bit nervous at all?"

"Who is making that wonderfully satisfying sound?"

And who do you suppose it was?

Ella, of course!